The Great Grizzly Race

By Zoa Lumsden

Illustrated by Monika Suska

If you travel far, far north, you will

find the wild land of Canada.

Watch out! Beware! Please take good care.

If you come here you might see a Grizzly Bear!

One lazy afternoon, the biggest, meanest Grizzly of all caught a weasel eating his berries. "Give me one good reason why I should not eat you?" roared the Grizzly.

"I have news of strangers!" squeaked the weasel.

"I saw two dogs on bikes."

"Strangers in MY valley?" said the Grizzly.

"Not for long!"

Nearby, the Dog Detectives,

Detective Jack and Deputy Poco,

were roasting marshmallows, when...

Out of the woodpile jumped Penny Beaver!

"Oww! Oww!" she yelled, "My tail is on FIRE!"

She put her tail in the river to put out the flames.

"Your campfire used to be my house!" said Penny.

"Now where will I hide?"

"What are you hiding from?" asked Deputy Poco.

"The biggest, meanest Grizzly of all," said Penny.

"That bully has stolen everyone's bikes so he can win

the great race."

"Jump on Penny!" said Detective Jack.

"We'll get your bikes back in time for the race."

The Dog Detectives rode off, deep into the valley.

They honked their horns and shouted, "Come out, everyone. Let us find the missing bikes!"

The animals searched until they found

a poop clue. Penny sniffed and sneezed,

"Achoooooo! Pepper always makes me sneeze."

"We must be getting close," said Deputy Poco.

"Only Grizzly poop has a peppery smell!"

The peppery poop trail led to muddy bicycle tracks.

But where were the missing bikes?

High above their heads, a duck said,

"Quack. Quack. QUACK!"

Everyone looked up and saw the bikes

hanging in the trees.

"Hot diggity hotdogs!" said Detective Jack.

"Let us get the bikes down before the Griz..."

The Grizzly let out a big ROAR! All of the
animals ran away except the Dog Detectives.

"I've met braver mice than you, Grizzly,"
said Detective Jack. "You stole everyone's bikes
because you are afraid to lose."

"I'm not afraid of anything," boasted the Grizzly.

"I'll see you wimps at the great race tomorrow!"

So the next morning, the riders were off

and the great race began.

Up, up and up they went. Who would win?

The Grizzly was fast and he took the lead.

But soon the Grizzly got tired and decided
to cheat. So at the top of the mountain,
he pushed over a tree.

What a disgrace! The Grizzly had ruined the race!

He whizzed down the mountain, ready to win.

But everything changed when he hit a huge...

....rock!

CRASH! SMASH!

The Grizzly cried out for help.

But... nobody wanted to help a bully.

"Come on," said Detective Jack. "Let us

show this Grizzly how good it feels to

have friends."

Together they pulled the Grizzly up.

For once, he did not try to bully them.

Instead, he smiled and cheered the

REAL winners of the Great Grizzly Race!

Quiz

1. What creatures must you beware of in the wildest wilderness?
a) Horses
b) Bears
c) Beaver

2. Where were the missing bikes?
a) Deep in a hole
b) Hidden in a shed
c) High in the trees

3. What does the Grizzly use to block the path during the race?
a) A tree
b) A rock
c) A bicycle

4. What animal has its tail on fire in the story?

a) A weasel

b) A beaver

c) A duck

5. Why does nobody want to help the Grizzly?

a) Because he is a bully

b) Because he is smelly

c) So that he does not win the race

Turn over for answers

Pink

Red (End of Yr R)

Yellow

Blue

Green

Orange

Turquoise (End of Yr 1)

Purple

Gold

White (End of Yr 2)

Lime

Book Bands for Guided Reading

The Institute of Education book banding system is made up of twelve colours, which reflect the level of reading difficulty. The bands are assigned by taking into account the content, the language style, the layout and phonics.

Children learn at different speeds but the colour chart shows the levels of progression with the national expectation shown in brackets. To learn more visit the IoE website: www.ioe.ac.uk.

Maverick early readers have been adapted from the original picture books so that children can make the essential transition from listener to reader. All of these books have been book banded for guided reading to the industry standard and edited by a leading educational consultant.

Quiz Answers: 1b, 2c, 3a, 4b, 5a